MORE
HOBO
STORIES

ART BURTON

DEDICATION

To Charley,

Abandoned on the side of the road
tied to a mailbox.

CONTENTS

ACKNOWLEDGMENTS

The ideas for stories in this book came from readers of *Hobos I Have Known* in most cases. I want to thank all those folks who took the time to tell me their stories.

As in the first book, I took these story ideas and ran with them. Every story has an element of truth, something that actually happened, in it, although the surrounding story and dialogue are in most cases totally made up. Sometimes I took two or more ideas and merged them into one story. I did this for you, the reader. Truth is stranger than fiction. Often the plain truth is so far out that people will say that could never have happened. As a result, I have added a touch of fiction to all these stories to make them more believable.

If I retold your story and you're thinking that's the not the way it happened, the changes were intentional. Eventually the Great Depression ended and many of these people settled in Nova Scotia to productive lives. Although by now, few of the actual hobos are still alive, their families still live in the area. For that reason I will throw in the disclaimer that none of the names or events represent any real person, living or dead. Any apparent connection is strictly coincidental. This is a work of fiction.

For those of you who read *Hobos I Have Known*, you will remember the narration is in a first person, female voice. The first four stories in this book follow that same policy with the same voice, for these are rural stories. The fifth story shows the exploits of another rural family with a different philosophy towards hobos. We switch to Truro for stories six and seven and then eight and nine are back to my female narrator on a farm somewhere in East Hants. Ten breaks the format and is a simple narration told by me, the author.

Thank you to Jay Underwood for the historical details about the railway trains travelling in Nova Scotia during the 1930s. If the facts didn't fit the story, literary licence stepped in. Sorry Jay.

As always, I must thank my wife, Flame, who served as a sounding board as I mulled over these stories, who went with me when I interviewed the people supplying the ideas, and who took the notes at these meetings to remind me what was said. I often got too caught up in the conversation to write anything down.

And once again, to all of you who contributed story ideas, I sincerely thank you. Without you, there would be no book.

The Knife Sharpener

The knock at the door came as no surprise. The train's whistle had sounded when I started clearing the table of the breakfast dishes. By now it was inevitable that a 'bo would soon be knocking. Ever since early 1930, hobos followed the arrival of the morning train like daylight follows the rising sun.

This time, however, it was different. The smiling face presented to me when I opened the door did not start with the usual "Can you spare a little food" line. Instead he said:

"I think I got here just in time."

I returned a confused look to this

comment.

From his pocket he withdrew a wooden-handled whetstone. "Ma'am, I'm here to sharpen your knives. I notice the bread on the table is sort of jagged where it has been sliced. Still tastes just as good, I'm sure, but makes it a lot harder on you. Dull knives increase the risk of being cut and injured. With all you have to do around this place, I'm sure you don't have time for that."

It took me a few seconds to process what he was saying. I glanced back at the table. Sure enough the stack of bread was sliced a little uneven. I could see the crumbs all over the counter where I hacked through the bread rather than cut through it. But me being injured by a dull knife, I gave him a skeptical look.

"And just exactly what can you do for me?" I asked, my voice dripping with sarcasm. After two years of these men showing up at my door, I had become comfortable with them. Some were all business: get some food and move on. Others were able to display their sense of humour and enjoyed a little kibitzing. I sensed this man fell into the latter category.

Again he proffered his whetstone. "Ma'am, I can make every knife in your drawers cut like a hot wire through butter." He smiled his winning smile. "And best of all, the first one is free. Get out your grimiest, dullest knife. The one you use to chip pieces off a stick of firewood to use as a wedge under your table leg and I will make it zing through anything better than it did when you first bought it. It can be Sheffield steel or a homemade blade made for you by your loving husband's hands."

Bought. That was a laugh. These knives had been in the family since the beginning of time passed down from generation to generation.

"The first one free sounds good," I said, "but after that, I'll tell you right up front, there's never been a surplus of money in this house and it hasn't gotten any better during the last few years. As for a husband, I've avoided those to date."

The man held up his hands to stop me. "A lady as attractive as you with no husband, I'm shocked. As for the lack of money, don't we all know about that," he said. "I'm not here to swindle you out of your last few pennies. A meal, some small change, and you'll think you have a complete set of new cutlery in your knife drawer. Let's do the free one and see where it goes from there."

I was pretty sure he was a flim-flam man, but what did I have to lose. I pulled out the drawer that held my knives, pawed through it until I found the one I used to cut the leaf and stock off my rhubarb. The sheer weight of the knife made it do its work and not the sharpness of the blade. Many a time it had been slammed into the ground so I would know where to find it and with the blade buried to the hilt in the soil so it wouldn't be cutting me.

He took the knife from my hand and smiled again.

"I've seen worse," he said, "but not by much."

I smiled back. "Well, can you make it like new or was that all talk?"

He laughed a deep, pleasant laugh. "A doubter. Have no fear, my trusty whetstone is up to any challenge. It can turn any piece of steel into a fine knife given enough time."

He looked in the direction of the stove. A pot of tea sat simmering on the back edge. "Perhaps, I could have a drop of tea to wet my whistle while my stone whets your blade."

"Payment in advance," I said as I got a cup down from the cupboard. "Now you will have to perform."

Again his wholesome laugh echoed throughout the kitchen. "Only a partial payment, I hope. When you see what your knife can do, you'll want to make me a full breakfast."

"Ah ha! So the first one isn't free. You expect breakfast in exchange."

He could tell I was teasing.

"You will be so impressed, you will insist I sit down for breakfast. I will refuse until I do more knives and earn that right. The first one is free and tea is just a product of your generosity. I can see your generous nature blossoming in your face, and yet no husband. It's a sign of the times. Who can afford to get married?"

We both laughed. If he could sharpen knives half as well as he could fling the blarney, I would have a new set of knives.

He took a sip of his tea and then his

face turned serious. He studied the beat-up knife I had presented to him from all sides before pouring a little tea from his cup onto the stone. The blade flashed back and forth, the pressure always being pulled back towards himself. The dirty edge started to reflect the light. Every so often, he paused to study his results before continuing.

He may have had the chatter of a con man, but there was no doubt he knew his craft. Soon the entire edge had taken on a metallic sheen. He stopped, held the knife up to his face, turned it one way and then the other and smiled.

"There," he said. He pulled up the sleeve of his shirt. Many little bare patches gave his arm a checkerboard look. He found a hairy spot and gently ran the blade along his arm. A spot of bare skin was left behind. He took another drink of his tea and looked at me for approval.

"Wow," was all I could think of to say. "I don't shave my arms, though. Let's see it slice this tomato."

I handed him a bright red, slightly overripe tomato. He set it on the table, slipped the point through the skin and cut off a one-eight inch slice. Then another and another and another and another.

"Perhaps a sandwich is in order," he said and looked at the bread on the plate in front of him.

A slid the plate towards him. "Go for it. I'm really impressed."

That was enough for him. His dazzling smile returned. "Can we do business?" he asked as he placed the four tomato slices onto the bread, added a little salt and pepper and took a bite.

The smile left my face. "As I told you earlier, money is not common in this house and what little there is, is not controlled by me."

He laughed. "Don't look so downcast. As the Good Book says 'money is the root of all evil.' I'm sure we can work something out."

As he was finishing this statement, the door behind him swung open and in walked my father. If there were decisions to be made about money, he would make them.

"That's not exactly what the Good Book says," he said as he stepped into the room. "The actual quote is: 'The love of money is the root of all evil.' What's going on here?" He looked at me for an answer.

"This man is a knife sharpener," I said, holding up the rhubarb knife. "Look what he did to this."

My father took the knife and rubbed his thumb across the blade. His forehead rose to express a little surprise. I could tell he was pleased with the results. As a rule, if a knife got really dull, he would have a go at it with mixed outcomes.

"We're trying to work out a deal to do the others, but I know we can afford to have it done." I took the knife back and examined it myself again.

My father pulled up a chair and sat down at the table. "Judging from your quote from First Timothy, there may be other possibilities besides exchanging cash. Is that correct?"

"Money is only useful for buying other things," the man said. "Perhaps we can skip that step and go right to the goods that money can purchase."

My father smiled. "I was going to have a cup a tea. You look like you could use more than a tomato sandwich. The slices look a little skimpy anyway." He looked at me. "Jean, that's no way to serve a sandwich. If you're going to cut them that thin, you may as well just leave them off and offer the man a slice of bread and butter."

I started to explain, but the hobo waved me off. "Pass me your knives while your father and I work out a deal. I'm sure we'll see eye to eye on something."

Before he left, I had a full drawer of razor-sharp knives. The hobo had a full breakfast of bacon, eggs and toast. In his sack, he carried some sandwiches for the road with the tomatoes cut twice as thick as the previous ones had been, new wool socks and a red and blue toque to keep his head warm during the upcoming winter. On his feet he sported another pair of wool socks replacing the memories of cotton socks that he has worn when he arrived.

My father finally had someone work for a meal without doing more damage than the meal was worth.

Everyone was happy.

Hot Potatoes

Could the strangers who roamed through our little villages and rural communities where your next door neighbour was two or three hundred yards or more up the road be trusted? Most times I would say definitely yes. Of course, there were the odd exceptions. If you've read *Hobos I Have Known* you know about the sock and mitten incident. It was going to be a cold winter in that case. In retrospect I can almost forgive that man.

Having said that, we did have another similar incident. By similar, I mean he wasn't stealing for personal gain, only for survival.

He had come later in the day than most 'bos who passed through our area. They usually arrived on the morning train which gathered the milk and dropped off the mail. It practically stopped in every backyard along the route. The afternoon train was more of an express and didn't stop as often.

The family had just seated itself around the dinner table when the slight knock came to the door. My father answered. He was the only one who could deliver strangers a pass to the evening meal in our house. Ordinarily these late arrivals would be fed outside and encouraged to move on. My father wasn't one to say no to someone in need, but he didn't want hobos sleeping in his barn. The best way to prevent that was to have them on their way again before they had a chance to ask. Giving them a takeout meal would be the modern day parlance.

Something about this little man must have piqued my father's curiosity because the next thing we knew, we were shuffling chairs around the table to make room for one more person. He was a slight man, probably in his mid-thirties to early forties and wearing a dark suit that had seen better days. Under the suit jacket he wore a heavy wool sweater. His brown hair leaned towards the long side but it looked like he attempted to finger comb it before knocking on our door.

The fare was simple enough that night. Boiled potatoes and carrots, both from our garden, a pork roast from a pig we had slaughtered earlier in the fall and the usual array of pickles, beets and homemade bread.

The meal was well underway before the man's arrival and as a result my brothers were pretty much finished as this man was just starting to chow down. He ravenously attacked the meal but you could tell he was uncomfortable in the presence of strangers. At the rate he was putting away the food, it wouldn't take him long to catch up to everyone else.

Before the stranger had joined us at the table, my father and brothers had been discussing where they were going to be cutting on the woodlot during the upcoming winter months, how much and what their plans were for the wood beyond our own use as a source of heat for the

next year. They fell back into this conversation and sort of forgot about our guest.

Earlier attempts to get him to talk and make him feel welcome could only be described as a failure. It was obvious the man had only one thing on his mind: filling the gap in his stomach. The others let him get on with that task and they returned to theirs.

In the kitchen, there were a couple of pies waiting to be served at the end of the meal. Supper wasn't a race in our family so no one minded waiting for everyone to finish before capping the meal with desert. No one had to rush off to watch *Jeopardy*. I excused myself to go out and start the preparation of the pies and to throw a handful of tea into the pot of boiling water.

When they talked about a certain area of the forest, I'm sure all of them could and did visual that exact piece of ground and had transported themselves there in their minds. They were lost in a tract of forest and not aware of what was happening at the table in our living room.

From my vantage point in the kitchen I could see our guest, but he would have to turn his head to see me. I watched as he focused his attention on my father, making sure he was lost in conversation with his sons. Meanwhile, his hand slowly crept across the table towards the dish of boiled potatoes. They still lived in their skins, because I figured everyone could easily peel their own potatoes and I had enough other things to do in the kitchen.

Then quick as a wink, his hand was back in his lap. I studied the bowl of potatoes. Was one missing? I wasn't sure. I always cooked extra potatoes for the evening meal and then had lots to make hash with the next day.

I stopped cutting up the pie with the blade of the knife still halfway through its stroke and watched. Slowly the hand went up to the table top. Again he stared at the boys as if their words flowed from the mouth of the Lord himself. And once again, just as quickly, his hand flashed back to his lap and then into the pocket of his suit coat. The bowl contained one less spud.

How many would he take? I wondered. How many would I let him take? As I said, these extra potatoes were destined to be fried up with a little bacon as hash for tomorrow's lunch. Both sides of the jacket seemed to be bulging slightly. One more, I told myself. I wanted to watch him do it again. But I was denied the chance. Either he had all he wanted or he detected a change in my father because a few seconds later, my dad turned towards him and asked him an innocent question that I could tell was just an attempt to include him in the conversation.

The man smiled, but did not reply. He knew nothing about forestry. I picked up the two pies, waltzed into the room, and with a flourish set them on the table. The hobo's eyes lit up at the sight of the pie and I could see him inhaling the spicy smell. Was he trying to figure out a way to add one of these slices to his pockets? No, but he definitely enjoyed the one he ate.

So was he stealing or just surviving. It was a cruel world during the depression and if he had put a couple more potatoes on his plate, mashed them up, added some salt and butter, no one would have questioned it. I certainly didn't begrudge him his "doggie bag."

Anything You Can Do

Although most of the people who showed up at our door were men, there were a few women. I'm not sure whether they could be called hobos or not. Some lived in the area, but took to the road in order to survive. If their husband was gone, they still had to eat. Often they would be dressed like a man and would try not to look too feminine. Like everyone else on the road, they just wanted to be fed and not to be hassled.

They were looking for work any where they could find it and offered a few different skills than their male counterparts. Most of them could pick berries or fruit with the best of the men and competed for these jobs. Other jobs, such as working on the roads, were considered male only territory. Women need not apply.

There were also women only areas of employment. Men could cook, clean and look after children, really they could, but were seldom considered for such positions. Each community would have a few men living alone who would employ women in these positions, usually for room and board. The jobs went to the local women, people the man knew and trusted. Jean, herself, held one of these positions in the story *New Boots* from *Hobos I Have Known*.

That being said, there were men in each community for whom no self-respecting woman would work. Their expectations included more than cooking and cleaning. Here, the travelling female hobos would have a chance of employment. How long she lasted would depend on how badly she needed the job, but even in these desperate times, some houses had a big turnover in workers.

These are not the hobos I'm talking

about in this story. I'm talking about the ones who hit the road going door-to-door like the men.

There was one woman, we'll call her Bessie, who could do anything a man could do. And when I say anything, I mean anything. I don't think she travelled on the trains like the other hobos because her hours were different. She would frequently show up at mid-day or in the early afternoon. As a result, my brothers got to know who she was. They worked in the barn doing morning chores when most of the hobos went by. They knew of these men, but seldom met them.

It didn't take Bessie long to become known in the community. She was a big lady, not fat, big. She wore a man's red and black checked hunting jacket over a sweater or two. This was common apparel for those not wearing suits of some sort. It depended on what kind of job you had lost and the Great Depression showed no favourites. It was an equal lack-of-opportunity employer.

Bessie wore lumberman rubbers on her feet and in those regards looked like any man. However, in between she still wore wool skirts that came to mid-calf. Usually it was dark brown or khaki suggesting she had once served in the WAAC or the women's auxiliary army corps near the end of the Great War.

If that was true, Bessie was used to competing against men in an unpopular role. The WAACs were never really accepted by many of the male soldiers at the time.

The mid part of the day on the farm was the break between the early morning chores and late afternoon chores. My brothers would usually be hanging around the house discussing what had already been done or what still had to take place. In the summer, this was the hottest part of the day and in the spring, the black flies could gang up and carry you away. It was not time to be in the fields of forests.

Like men in general, these guys could be unintentionally cruel to people in dire straits. They like to show off to each other and often made witty, or so they thought, remarks at the expense of others. When it came to Bessie, my father didn't tolerate this. He recognized that if survival was tough for a man out there on the road, it had to be even more of a challenge for a woman. He tried to keep my brothers in check.

Bessie did not make that easy. She was her own woman and had no concerns about how others saw her. She wasn't a trouble maker; she was hungry. She would knock on the door and no matter how often, we would invite her inside, she would decline. Perhaps this was for the best. Among her habits was the use of tobacco. Not the smoking kind, the chewing kind.

One could only chew for so long before the necessity of spitting came up. Here Bessie was both considerate and crude at the same time. She didn't simply let fly like some men did. Bessie would be standing on our side porch waiting patiently for a sandwich, afternoon fare was the same as morning fare: eggs on toast, when the urge to spit would hit her.

Without giving the matter any thought, she would slide the rug that lie outside our door aside and spit on the step and then slip the rug back into place hiding the offending brown gob of mangled tobacco juice. My brothers were hard pressed to keep from laughing when this happened and frequently failed in their efforts.

My father, either never saw Bessie perform this trick or chose to ignore it. Latter in the day, the boy who laughed the loudest would be tasked to go out and wash the steps and porch deck. Even this didn't silence the laughter every time it happened. Bessie was a regular who showed up at least once a month or so.

Spitting on the step wasn't Bessie's best trick for breaking up the decorum of my brothers. As I said earlier, she could do anything a man could do, anything. After getting a sandwich and a cup of tea, she would take her leave. Half-way down the driveway, Mother Nature would always seem to make a call on her. She must have had a small bladder.

Bessie would step off into the ditch, with her back to the house, she would hike up her skirt and answer that call as effectively as any may ever did. The boys would be rolling on the floor in laughter.

I'm pretty sure if we could see Bessie's face there would be a big smile there as well, a little performance to bring joy to the lives of others during tough times. It cost her nothing and she was always welcomed and fed when she showed up at our door.

A Twist of Fate

Trains and hobos seem to go together and for good reason. These lumbering steel giants that snaked their way throughout the countryside were an ideal way for getting from one part of the country to another with very little effort on the part of the traveller. It's not that the trains make an effort to go through all these small towns and villages; the small towns and villages sprung up like dandelions in spring along the expanse of the train's route.

As romantic as it may sound to hop a train in one town and jump off a couple of hundred miles down the way, there were risks involved.

Basically trains allowed three methods of free travel. All had their advantages and all had their risks. Being caught and arrested was one downside of stealing a ride. These were law-a-biding men with no desire to spend the night in the local lockup with drunks and criminals.

To prevent that, many hobos would climb up to the top of the train and lie down out of sight. Not even the keenest railroad dick would bother checking the roofs of the cars unless he could do so from a vantage point high above them.

There were problems with this hideout. You were exposed to the elements and the wind and the never-ending cloud of coal smoke coming from the engine which trailed directly down the path of the train. This choking smoke made this method undesirable.

Of course inside the car held many advantages if you could find one that wasn't locked. You were out of the weather; you were out of sight; and because you didn't have to hold on, you could sleep away the hours. The above mentioned railway police kept a close watch on these locations and if caught there was no escape. You could end up in jail.

Also other hobos might be territorial about these locations and fights could ensue about who could share a car. Knocking on someone's door looking for food was always a crap shoot. Showing up with cuts, bruises and black eyes lessened your changes of success.

Under the car was the final travel spot. In fact this is where the expression riding the rods comes from. Break rods were slung under the car creating a place to squeeze into. If traveling from town to town was your goal and not comfort, this could be a good place to be. Here you were tucked out of sight of prying eyes. You were out of the weather and there was little competition for these spots.

The down side here was obvious. Lose hold of your grip and you're lying on the rail bed between two sets of thundering steel wheels. Lose your head in this situation and you could quite literally lose your head or some other body part. Falling asleep was not an option.

When we look back at that age of

travelling men who crisscrossed the country, we often don't realize that everyday was a battle for survival. We tend to forget that if they could find no food, they went hungry. This is what led them to the desperation of stealing rides on trains, despite the risks, to get to new areas of opportunity.

This brings me to my story. I boarded my train in Truro, as a paying customer, for an exciting and never before made trip to Halifax. I had been visiting relatives in the hub town for a couple of weeks when the idea of the journey cropped up. It took almost all of the money I had saved up for me to join my two cousins on this journey. I could hardly wait to see the big city, although I must admit there was some trepidation on my part. All those people, all those cars that I had read about.

Where I lived we could count the number of automobiles you would see in a week on the fingers of one hand. In the city, you would have to stand at the side of the road and wait for several minutes to get a chance to cross and then risk your life by running as fast as you could to the other side, or at least that's what I had been told. It was scary just thinking about it.

The train we chose to take our adventure had originated in Montreal and was badly mis-named *The Maritime Express*. There was nothing express about it. It seemed we stopped in everyone's backyard and often hung around long enough to chat and have a cup of tea while we were there. Maybe my excitement about going to the city made they trip seem longer than it actually was.

However, all that changed when we reached Shubenacadie. As the trains started to slow down, a slur of red liquid shot across the window a few seats ahead of me. Everyone in the area jumped back in surprise. Then the viscous, crimson fluid slowly ran down the panes of glass. Seconds later the train jolted to a stop, almost knocking us from our seats.

People outside came running from every direction towards our part of the train. Excitement and concern seemed to combine to make up their demeanor. Some men ran right up to our car and out of our sight they were so close, but most hung back about twenty feet or so.

We flattened our noses against the window to see the object of all this sudden interest. By then the action was behind us. Word filtered from the front of the train that a man had jumped from a boxcar, staggered back, fell and had his arm severed clean off. The red stuff on the window came from that arm. Everyone moved back.

My cousins and I looked at each other with the same question in our eyes: Should we get off and investigate? We all wanted to, but no one made the first move. Finally we decided to stay where we were.

Suddenly people were pointing out the window again. We could see a tight knot of men running past carrying something.

Before we could figure out what it was the train started to move. Slowly at first and then it revved up to a speed that we hadn't experienced all the way from Truro. We sat back in stunned silence as the countryside whizzed by us.

Stations landings along the way contained confused people wondering why their ride hadn't stopped. We could see their heads turning to follow our path and then quickly disappear from sight. Some had raised their hands in a stopping motion and were left standing with their hands still in the air.

In no time we were sweeping by a huge expanse of water. A few minutes previously, we had passed Grand Lake, but this was even bigger.

"Bedford Basin," my cousin said. He had made this trip before. "We're almost there."

"Almost where?" I asked.

"Halifax," he said. "We came directly to the city. Wow, that was fast."

And indeed, we had made the trip non-stop. It turns out the local doctor, known to most everyone as Dr. Mac was at the station waiting for his aged mother who was returning from a trip to Montreal. As soon as he saw the commotion, he hustled down to the crowd of people and took charge.

We were later told that he whipped off his belt and made a tourniquet around the hobo's remaining stub of an arm. He then commandeered the train to make the direct trip to the city hospitals. The engineers had never run across a situation like this before. Rather than argue, they followed the doctor's instructions. In no time at all the poor man found himself at the Victoria General Hospital in south end Halifax.

I would like to say the story had a happy ending, but that was not the case. The doctors succeeded in saving the man's life, but that turned out to be the least of his problems. Unable to find work before the accident, he became definitely unemployable with only one arm.

Stories would drift back to Shubenacadie, his hometown from time to time and from there filter back to our little community. The initial publicity gave him a little notoriety and for a while he was looked after by curiosity seekers. Soon that wore thin and he found himself living on the streets in Halifax struggling by as best as he could. He became one of the many looking for handouts and hand ups.

Believing life had dealt him a bad hand, and who could argue with that, he became argumentative, hostile and difficult to get along with. Everyone shunned him, even his fellow street people.

The last I heard, he had frozen to death one cold winter night on Spring Garden Road, near the Public Gardens. This big life change was caused by one little twist of an ankle jumping from a train in his hometown. He jumped off early because sometimes the police were waiting to catch hobos jumping down from the cars.

That seldom happened in Shubenacadie. They had no police force of their own. He had, it turned out, spend too much time in the bigger cities to remember the relaxed way of life back home, a place were people looked after each other whoever they happened to be.

Unfortunately he couldn't handle that kind of life. He preferred to live amongst strangers, rather than take handouts from friends. I'm in no position to judge, I've never walked in those shoes, but in the end that turned out to be a fatal decision.

Roadside Fare

"Hey, kids. Come here. The train is coming."

My mother's words were becoming a common anthem in recent weeks. Every train that chugged through our little village seemed to carry more and more of the transient men seeking work in the area and beyond. Few were burdened with money in their pockets and they relied on the generosity of the local residents to feed them. Hobos became the accepted terminology to describe these seekers of food.

I lived on a farm with three sisters and my mother and father. My father frequently worked in either the distant fields or back on the woodlot gathering fuel for the winter furnace or to sell if he could find a market. Although some families allowed these hobos onto their doorsteps to eat, my Aunt Jean even fed them at her table, my mother preferred they stay off our property completely. She wasn't a prude. With a houseful of females, she was cautious. Her caution was encouraged by my sisters and me.

Still, she was as willing as anyone to share our good fortune. We didn't have money to speak of, but we were never without food. Hard work by my parents saw to that. We all did our fair quota of work in the gardens during the planting in the spring, weeding in the summer and harvesting in the fall to keep our larder filled to overflowing. There was plenty to spare and my mother was willing to split it with those in need. In truth, as the Depression continued into the thirties, we planted and raised more vegetables and animals with this thought in mind. It was the least we could do. Ironically, it was the most we could do as well. We could not offer these men employment for wages.

My father had little faith in the claims of the politicians of the day who promised things would be better next year. They never were, at least not until the war put everyone back to work or sent them overseas to die. Anyway, I digress. Sitting at the supper table with my father for all those years hammered his cynical views into my head.

One more thing. I don't want to give the impression that my mother was the only one afraid of these men. She wasn't. The first time one of them showed up on our doorstep, my sisters and I all ran upstairs and hid. We didn't know what was going on when grubby strangers started coming to our door begging for food.

In our little community, we knew everybody and if we searched hard enough, we could find some way in which we were related. "Who's your father?" was a popular way for people from neighbouring communities to start a conversation.

We lived a little ways from the railway tracks and up a steep driveway. As a result, not many of the hobos actually came to our house. My father came up with an idea to prevent any of them from coming. Well, preventing is not the right word, he discouraged them from coming up to our house, but in a good way.

When we heard the train whistle, and it went through every day, my mother made part of a loaf of bread into sandwiches. We kids would deposit it on a tray at the end of our driveway that my father had built. It was about two feet square with a cover to protect it from the rain. If the hobos were slow in coming, the crows would soon clean up the food.

The first few times Dad walked down the driveway with us. The closer we got to the tray, the more fearful we became and tried to hang back.

"No one's going to hurt you," my father said, pulling on our hands. "Stop acting so silly. Be thankful you don't have to rely on the generosity of strangers to get your meals."

We nodded our heads in agreement, but were still afraid. When he stopped walking us down, we would creep cautiously down the driveway for the first two-thirds, then run the last few feet, throw the sandwiches onto the tray and run all the way back up the driveway as fast as we could.

It didn't take the men long to figure out that this was as far as they were to come. Most would take one or two sandwiches and move on. We watched from a bedroom window facing the road. The odd one would take them all; stuff everything into his pockets and take off while scanning the area all around to see if someone was watching. They were the exceptions.

Of course we didn't do this everyday. It would depend on what else had to be done on that day and eventually we girls would be on the train ourselves going to the high school in Windsor. At first I was scared when I knew I would be taking the same train as these men to get to school. My fears were unfounded. Never in all the years I attended high school did I see what you would call a hobo in the passenger car.

My mother was skeptical of my father's plan at first.

"What happens on the days we don't put anything out?" she asked. "They'll be mad and will be up here banging on our door."

Father gave her a knowing smile, this infuriated her, and said: "Don't worry, if there's no food on the tray they will simply move on." He gave his head a firm nod as he said this. "They have a secret code," he assured her. "If there is nothing on the tray, the others will know not to come to the house."

"Don't be foolish," my mother said. "Every day, the train brings a different batch of men. They don't talk to each other. They don't even see each other."

Once again, my father gave her his infuriating smile. "That's all true," he agreed, "but somehow they do communicate. They always go to your sister Jean's house, but never go to Enos Blandford's house just down the road, because he never feeds them. Put sandwiches out when you can and on the other days no one will bother us. I promise."

And you know what, he was right.

The Baloney Sandwich

Mary looked out through the kitchen window to see who was knocking on the door. She showed no surprise when she observed a man in old, worn clothes with a downcast look on his face. There had been a steady stream of hobos following the arrival of every train in the downtown Truro area for the past six months. Mary knew the whistle of the train was the precursor to a knock on her door and had heard its blast ten minutes earlier.

Recently the stock market had crashed in New York followed by downturns in the economies of countries around the world.

Although few, if any, of these men showing up at her door had ever owned any stocks, they soon became the victims of the bad times of those who had. Factory gates were being locked across the country, throwing thousands of men out of work. This displaced workforce soon became a mobile wave looking for work anywhere they could find it.

Mary opened the door. On the doorstep sat a glass bottle filled with milk delivered a few minutes earlier by the Scotsburn milkman. Fifteen cents, a dime and a nickel, balanced on the top of the cardboard cover. Mary had left a quarter in the empty bottle the night before. She scooped the two coins from the bottle top and into the pocket of her apron. The hobo watched the action, but said nothing until Mary looked at him.

Then the oft heard statement of recent times came from his lips. "Morning, Missus. You couldn't spare a little food for a hungry traveller?"

Unlike several people during this year of 1930, Mary's husband still had a good paying job. When the Great Depression hit the world the year before, Mary and her family had been spared the worst of it. She wasn't sure if she felt guilt from her good fortune or if she strongly believed the Bible's imperative to be her brother's keeper. Regardless, no one was turned away during these increasingly troubled times.

"Have a seat here on the step and I'll bring you a sandwich. Do you like bologna?"

His eyes lit up at the mere mention of the word. "Boloney? Lord tundering, Luv, I 'aven't 'ad a good boloney sandwich since boardin' da boat from Newfoundland to Canada. Please 'n t'ank you, dat would be lovely." He hesitated. "P'raps a wee cup of tea might 'company dat offerin'. It don't 'ave to be fresh, Darlin'. If d'ere's a wee spot left in da pot from breakfast it would do just grand. I likes it strong."

Mary couldn't help smiling at the man's enthusiasm.

The hobo responded to her smile with one of his own, obviously encouraged by Mary's friendly attitude. "I don't want to impose, Missus, but when my dear departed Ma, God rest her soul, served us boloney, she always dropped it into a hot pan for a wee bit on each side." His smile widened at the memory. "And den she would put a daub of yeller mustard on it." The smile instantly dropped from his face. "But just plain boloney on bread would do me right up. I don't wants to ask too much."

Mary laughed, despite her efforts not to. "I think I can find some mustard somewhere and I'm sure a hot meal will hit the spot more than a cold one." The man's rolling accent and twinkling eyes captivated her. She fingered the fifteen cents in her pocket as she returned to the kitchen to fill the food order.

She took the roll of Maple Leaf bologna from the ice box, cut off a slab and dropped it into her cast iron frying pan with a little butter. Three quick slashes to keep the meat from curling and she turned to the breadbox. From a freshly-made loaf of bread, she hacked off two thick slices and slathered butter on them. She flipped the bologna in the pan and then dropped it onto one slice of bread. She found a jar of mustard in the cupboard and applied the yellow substance to the other slice. Satisfied with her creation, she wrapped it in a piece of newspaper and took it to the man waiting patiently on her back step.

The obvious pleasure on his face made the extra effort worthwhile. "I've got some tea brewing on the stove. It should be ready by now," she said.

Mary returned to the kitchen, poured the brown liquid into a cup, added some of the newly purchased milk and a teaspoon of sugar. She paused for a few seconds and then prepared a cup for herself. She took both cups to the back porch and leaned on the railing while the man scarfed down his sandwich. Trails of mustard bordered both sides of his mouth.

Mary made an unconscious wiping motion at the sides of her own mouth. The hobo noticed her actions and followed suit. He looked at the yellow stain on the tips of his fingers and wiped them off on the remaining bite of sandwich. He then popped it into his mouth before taking his first drink of tea.

Mary noticed the hesitation on his face as he sipped. "Is it sweet enough?" she asked.

"T'is fine, Luv" the man replied, "just fine."

Then she remembered his claim that old tea would be fine. He liked it strong. The sugar had been an added bonus she could have done without.

"Let me get you another cup without sugar," she said.

The man took a full mouthful and swallowed. "No, Luv, dis is the finest t'ing. T'ank you kindly."

He was adamant so Mary let it go. She took a slurp of her own tea before asking: "Where are you going from here?"

The man returned his cup to the saucer. "I 'ear dere's work in da Valley pickin' berries–strawberries and blueberries both–den in da fall ... apples. Work should find me all summer if luck comes me way."

Luck will have nothing to do with it, Mary thought. This man's pleasant disposition and eagerness to please should land him a job in no time. After that, it was up to him, but if she were any judge of character, this man looked like he would carry his own share of the work load and guarantee he would be kept on for the duration.

He set down his cup and got to his feet. Mary noticed half the tea still remained. If you like your tea black, any amount of sugar is too much her husband had once told her. She set down her own cup as the man turned to leave.

"I wants to t'ank you, Missus," he said. "Dat fried boloney warms me spirit as well as me belly. God bless ya, Luv."

As she climbed the steps back to the kitchen, she heard the two coins in her pocket rattle together. She reached in and pulled them out. "Here, take this..." she said, "for a tea or ... another sandwich along the way."

The man studied the offering then shook his head. "Oh no, Missus. Da sandwich was perfect, more dan expected. T'ank ya kindly."

Mary was not to be denied. She reached out and took the man's rough hand and forced the coins into it. "I insist. Get yourself a good cup of tea later."

Tears formed at the corners of the man's eyes. A look of genuine gratitude embraced his body. His voice took on a serious tone. "T'ank ya, Missus. T'ank ya kindly. Nothin' makes a good day better like a hot cup of tea when a dry t'irst grasps you by da t'roat. I sees you're a lady who would understand t'at. I'll be remembering yc when I 'as it." He swiped at his eyes with the back of his hand; then his radiant smile once again swept over his facial features.

"Enjoy it," Mary said and turned before her own tears started to flow. It was only fifteen cents but the joy she could see on the man's face was worth a million dollars.

The Full Meal Deal

In most cases these roving men who came knocking on the doors of folks here in the Maritimes were fed on the doorstep. Sometimes, they made it as far as the kitchen table as you saw in the first hobo book, *Hobos I Have Known.*

The train would come into a community and all those hiding onboard would disperse to the various houses in the area where they knew a meal could be had. They would try not to hit the same house over and over on the same day. They realized there were going to be others following them and it was important they have places where they would be accepted.

People were willing to help out, but everyone has a breaking point when they say "enough is enough."

There existed at least one house in Truro, Nova Scotia where this was not the case. The travellers were invited in and treated as proper guests in large numbers.

The house was near the Parkland Bridge and right in the line of sight of the railroad tracks. The engine of the train stopped a little farther up the line, but the rail cars would continue down as far as the bridge. As you know from these stories, riding the rails was the preferred way of travel for these unemployed wanders seeking work wherever they could find it. If not preferred, it was definitely the most common.

The lady of the house in question, we'll call her Marie, knew why these men were on the move. She knew they weren't vagabonds as we understand the term — beggars of food and money. They were victims of the greatest depression to hit the world since the 1870s. They were seeking employment in any place they could find it. There purses, if they carried one, had long since been depleted of cash.

They were at the mercy of the community through which they were travelling and had to resort to begging for a meal, any kind of meal.

Marie understood this. Once a week, Sunday, she wanted to give these men a respite in the miserable circumstances in which they found themselves. She knew when the trains would pass through town and she knew when the hobos would be on board. She was prepared.

She would lay out the table in the dining room with a proper table cloth. She would use real silverware and dishes that matched. And most importantly, she prepared home cooked meals, not simply a sandwich, but a meal. No meal is complete without dessert. Marie made pies. Pies were a distant memory for some of these men. Often she would notice tears in their eyes as she slipped a slice of apple pie onto the plate in front of them.

These meals would be a one time adventure for these men. They were passing through. One meal and on the road again unless they found employment in the area. If that happened, many of them would remember this meal as a turning up point in a life that only contained downturns in the last few years. They would remember Marie.

A lot of us eat on the run in this new fast-paced-age. Getting the family together happens on Thanksgiving or Christmas. In past times, the evening meal was the highlight of the day for the family. It gave them all a chance to come together and discuss what had taken place in their lives that day.

For these road warriors trying to eke out an existence anyway they could, one of the things they missed most was the family meals. Not just the food, they were still being fed. They missed the camaraderie of relaxing over a meal and enjoying the conversation of others.

This was the other thing Marie offered. It was not always easy to generate. At the start of each meal, shovelling in the food while keeping a watchful eye on those around you was the normal practice. Most of these men were strangers to each other, even if they appeared to be travelling together.

Marie would act as the catalyst for discussion.

"So, where are you from?" she would ask one.

"What did you do before the big crash?" she would ask another.

They would look up from their meals with a surprised look on their face. Very few people had taken an interest in them as a person for a long time. Often they were looked upon as a nuisance who had to be fed because the person's Christian upbringing demanded they be their brothers' keeper, but they didn't have to enjoy it.

"I'm from Mabou on Cape Breton Island," one would answer.

Another would look up. "Mabou? Do you know Donnie MacDonald. I worked with him a couple of weeks ago in Tatamagouche. He was from Mabou."

The first guy would laugh. "Donnie MacDonald. That's the name of half the population. How old was he? I bet you mean Donnie the mechanic. He was in Tatamagouche the last time I went through there."

And the ice would be broken and conversation would flow. Suddenly, these men were back at their own dining room tables just shooting the breeze with a bunch of friends. They would talk about their former jobs, places they had been, the political situation, funny stories they had heard, anything and everything. For a short time they could forget about the fact that they didn't know where there next meal would come from or when. After the pie was all gone, they would offer to help clean up because they now felt like part of a family again.

Marie always turned them down. That's how she was able to serve the meal on matching dishes. Only she would handle them while they were slippery and soapy.

Marie was doing God's work, although she didn't dwell on that thought. That might lead to pride. Instead she accepted that she was simply a servant of the Lord doing what the Bible taught: looking out for her fellow man in the best way she could.

Rising from the Ashes

Jean walked out the door of her neighbour's kitchen, a tray of sandwiches in her hands. Her eyes took in the new barn growing out of the field beside the house. Several men kneeled on the roof putting the finishing touches on the new asphalt shingles covering the barn's gambrel roof. They were working on the upper part of the double sloped surface. The echoing of their hammers created a symphony of percussion instruments filling the air with sounds of hard work in progress. From Jean's position on the ground, the hunched over men looked like raccoons scurrying across the roof.

Traces of scorching highlighted some of the dried, dead grass around the base of the barn.

As she watched, a few of the men stopped hammering and sat back on their haunches. Soon, only Rob Mcdonald still actively hammered shingles into place. Rob, perched on the peak of the roof, added the final touches to the wrapped shingles that joined the two sides of the barn.

His previous barn had been shingled with wooden shakes. This time he wasn't fooling around. The new asphalt singles were supposed to be fire resistant, whatever that meant. He hoped it meant he wouldn't have to go through this ever again. When he reached the far right of the peak, he stopped, looked at the other men and smiled.

"Gentlemen, this is it. One more nail and the barn is finished." With a flourish, he knocked the last nail into place. The others threw their hats into the air and scooted their butts towards the waiting ladders. A new, bright red barn now filled the space recently occupied by a charred black scar in the barnyard. Rob Mcdonald was back in the business of farming.

His barn and his house had fallen victim to an intense fire only three months earlier. The generally accepted conclusion throughout the community suggested the fire was caused by a passing hobo smoking in the barn. A hobo Rob had authorized to spend the night there.

The hobo had arrived on the same day that the last of the season's hay had been loaded into the loft. Rob's wife, Nancy, fed the man, as was the custom, during this period of the early '30s. Two fried eggs and a cup of tea had filled the empty spot in the man's belly and brought a smile to his haggard face.

The so-called Great Depression had wiped out the employment of thousands of people throughout the country, throughout the world for that matter. Several of these men had gone in search of work wherever the rumours said it existed.

Their favourite form of transport became the slow moving freight trains crawling through the countryside. Their frequent stops, especially in rural areas where the trains gathered and delivered both mail and milk, made them easy to jump on and off. One such drop-off point, a station about one-half mile down the road, could be easily seen from the roof of Rob's new barn. The sight haunted him all through the building process.

After having finished the egg sandwich Nancy presented to him, the hobo asked Rob if he could lay his head down in the barn for the night.

He pointed to the sky. "Those clouds building in the west suggest we're in for a wet one before morning."

That would be the old barn. Initially, Rob had balked at the idea.

"The barn's filled with fresh, new hay and any sort of spark could set it ablaze."

The hobo had vigorously shaken his head. "No problem there, my friend. I don't smoke. Who can afford tobacco and papers these days." He had laughed. This was an argument the hobo had heard several times in the past and his defensive lines were delivered smoothly. He had used them many times before.

Rob looked up at the sky. He had put on a big drive to get his haying finished that day. As the hobo had said, all the signs pointed to an upcoming rain storm. The threatening clouds had precipitated Rob's final burst of energy to get his haying finished for the season. Reluctantly, against his better judgment, he agreed to allow the man to spend the night nestled into the freshly mown hay and out of the weather.

"I knew better," Rob said later, unable to hide the self-disgust in his voice. "I asked the son of a coon dog if he smoked. He laughed and assured me he didn't. Couldn't afford to buy tobacco he said. Then he burns down not only my barn but also my house. The lying scoundrel."

Indeed that was the truth. Rob heard a huge commotion in the middle of the night, snapping and cracking of burning timbers. A reddish glow danced on his bedroom window. He scrambled from his bed and was met by the sickening sight of flames shooting through the roof of his barn and lighting up the night.

Several neighbours appeared with buckets, but to no avail. The heat generated by the raging fire prevented them from getting close enough to put the buckets to effective use. By the time daylight arrived the next morning, not only was the barn a pile of rubble, but so were his house, carriage shed and chicken coop. The yard looked like a war zone. The hobo was no where to be seen. Adding to the mess, soon after dawn, the rain arrived in torrents. Too late to help with the actual fire, but successful in dousing the remaining hotspots in the foundations and making everything a soupy mess.

Rob and Nancy had lived on the farm with their nine children. Now their house was beyond repair. Looking out for his family gave Rob little time to mourn the loss of his farm. He had to find a place for everyone to live or he would be joining the hobos going door to door himself.

On the bright side, none of his cows had been in the barn when the flames engulfed it. On the warm summer evenings they preferred to be out in the open fields. His source of income was intact. On the down side, all of next winters feed had fueled the fire and caused the rapid spread as the swirling wind generated by the fire sent the clumps of flaming hay from building to building, torching them in the process. If only the rain had come four hours earlier, things might not have been so bad.

The hobos frequented this country area because the people believed in looking out for their fellow man. The help they offered to strangers paled beside the support offered to one of their own. Before Rob had cleaned the black grime from his face, all of his children had found places to stay and he and Nancy were offered several places of refuge.

They took up their friend's offers. The youngest children moved in with him and Nancy at her brother's nearby farm. The older kids bunked in with close-by neighbours allowing them to retain some sense of family.

The process of rebuilding began the next day. Most of the local farmers had put on the same drive as Rob to get their haying finished. They had time available they claimed. The Co-op insurance man showed up later that afternoon and authorized the building products they would need. Most of the men in the neighbourhood arrived with their own hammer and saws. In a little over a month the family reunited in the new house standing on the foundation of the old one.

Next the workforce turned to replacing the barn. These men may not have been carpenters, but they had all had a hand in raising barns. There were a couple of them who knew how to build square buildings with equal sides, not as easy as you might think. The gambrel roof's trusses required some knowledge. Many of these type barns had been build in the area before. Each man knew what had to be done and did it. And now here was Rob sitting on the roof hammering in the final nail.

Jean moved forward with her tray of food.

"Anyone hungry?" she asked.

They answered with a resounding chorus of yeses. Each man grabbed a sandwich as he stepped off the ladder from the roof and gobbled it down as voraciously as any of the passing hobos had ever devoured theirs. He then grabbed another from the plate and moved on. A bucket of water with a couple of dippers sat on the ground beside her. Condensation coated the side of the bucket. They slurped up this cold water from deep down in the bowels of the earth and nothing tasted better.

Many removed their caps and mopped the perspiration from their heads and looked back up at the sun drenched roof. There was handshaking and back patting all around. They were swollen with the pride of a job well done and rightly so. What had been a scar on the earth three months earlier was now a proud new factory to produce milk, cream and cheese. A family was reunited and a party was about to begin.

Several of the local women were busy in their own kitchens preparing for the party which would run long in to the night. All barn raisings ended with a barn dance and this one would be no exception. Under the circumstances, this party promised to be the most exciting ever.

Rob was the last to jump down from the ladder. He took in the sight of his fellow workers. "I don't know how to thank you for all your help." His voice choked up a little. "You've renewed my faith in mankind." He hesitated for a few seconds, fighting back tears welling in the corner of us eyes, looking for additional words of thanks. Then a huge smile lit up his face. "Oh hell, break out the fiddles and let's party. We deserve it."

Caught Short

Most of these hobos who came to our door were looking for food and nothing else. But, occasionally they would want an extra service. Eating food leads to another bodily function that can't be ignored. Mostly these men would make use of the sides of the road or the woods around the railway tracks. I state that as fact but have no idea if it's true; it just makes sense.

Letting go in the wide open spaces as opposed to letting go cooped up inside a stinking little building seems to be no contest.

On a couple of occasions, the urge to

go hit a man with such force that he couldn't wait to get back to the privacy of the woods. Our driveway was over one hundred yards long and when your bowels were boiling, you overcame your shyness and asked to use the facilities. Outhouse, biffy, john, can, toilet, there were no shortages of designations. They all meant the same thing on our farm, a little red and white building up by the barn.

It was reasonable close to the house and even while you squeezed your butt cheeks together, you could get there fairly quickly. Barn odours, outhouse odours, at least they were all in the same place.

We did have some hazards on the way, though. Several clothes lines ran from the corner of an outbuilding that housed our fanning mill to the corner of the barn. They hung just high enough so that I, at five feet four inches, could reach up and hang clothes on them. Most of my family were short enough to walk under them. George had to duck slightly. If you stayed on the path they offered no problems until you got near the barn and then you went under them.

There were four of these lines, no

pulleys for us although I had seen pictures of those new devices that allowed you to hang out your clothes from one spot. Most days, if the sun was shinning, something would be hanging from at least one of these lines.

This was late in the year and the man had arrived at supper time. He was tall and lanky, wore a suit coat with at least one sweater under it. A stocking cap covered his ears. The sun had set early that night; there was a heavy cloud cover. Darkness had set in. My father had invited him to join us at the table and he had happily accepted even though he was not what you would call chatty. He was there for the food, make no mistake about that. His hat went into his coat pocket.

I served him that evening's fare, eggs poached in tomato soup served in a bowl on toasted, homemade bread. He looked skeptical but dug in anyway. Food was food. We were all eating the same thing. The slight smile on his face indicated his acceptance of this new-to-him dish. He said nothing.

Then his head popped up with a pained expression. His hands went to his belly and there was a rumbling sound. He looked at my dad almost afraid to mumble the words but had to get them out.

"Can I use your outhouse?" He was already starting to stand up. He let out a low, moaning groan.

Dad, for his part, quickly recognized the problem and slid back his chair and guided the man to the door. He pointed in the general direction of our privy.

"Right up there at the left corner of the barn," he said. "White door with a little moon. Can't miss it."

Dad stepped back into the house. He thought his instructions were perfectly clear and to the point. He had just sat down when we heard the first scream. All of us looked towards the door.

"Don't think he made it," my brother chuckled. Dad gave him a burnishing look. He started for the door.

The next scream sent chills down our back. Dad started running. We all got up to follow.

The third scream had words attached. "Let go of me! Let go! Let go!"

I thought I could make out a flash of white in the darkness.

"Help me! Help me-e-e-e!" Was the man being attacked by some kind of animal?

My brother George flew past my dad up the path to the barn.

"Someone get a lantern," he called back to us and then faced forward and yelled: "Relax. What's wrong."

Both George and Dad disappeared into the gloom.

A lantern hung by the door along with a container of matches. On nights like this, the lantern always went to the outhouse with us. Dad didn't think this man had time to bother with light or maybe the thought of a light simply never occurred him, I'm not sure which. Lester started up the path surrounded by a yellow glow. He held the lantern high over his head.

The screaming sounds continued to assault our ears. It almost sounded like a fight was taking place out there in the darkness. George would quickly put a stop to that, I thought. Lester hustled up the path and forms of men started to take shape in the darkness. I could only make out three and recognized them all, Dad,

George and Lester. What had happened to the hobo?

George's laughter came first. "Settle down, settle down," he said between bursts of laughter. He seemed to kneel down. "Stop struggling. It's all right." He said this in a loud voice that would freeze anyone to their spot.

"Hold still," my father's voice carried down to us. Even his voice carried a degree of mirth.

We all started up the path. We had grabbed and lit another lantern. When we got there, we understood the reason for the laughter, but before we could join in my father admonished us not to make a sound.

The man lay on the ground under the second clothesline. A white sheet flapped in the breeze over him, but that wasn't what brought out the laughter from George. A suit of red flannel underwear was tangled around the hobo. The arms of the suit wrapped around his neck, the legs clung to his body. A red scratch lined his forehead at what would have been the height of the clothesline, the first blow in the ensuing battle.

The man looked around himself in the lantern light. "Something grabbed me," he said. The fear was still evident on his face. "Grabbed me and wouldn't let go."

He still didn't realize he had lost a battle with a set of combination underwear.

"Do you still have to go to the outhouse?" Dad asked. He took Lester's light. "Here take this." He turned to the rest of us. "Get back down to the house and finish your supper. This young fellow will join us shortly."

He didn't. Did he relieve his bowels before, during or after the fight with the underwear? We never found out. George's red flannels disappeared as well. Eventually Dad retuned to the table.

"The gentleman is feeling under the weather," he said. "He won't be rejoining us. What's for desert?"

He had closed the case. No further discussion of the underwear-hobo fight followed. At least not that night.

Not Really a Survivor

I shuddered as the eerie noise wafted up from the railway tracks. It reverberated through my brain like the sound of a cat in heat or an animal stuck in a leg-hold trap preparing to gnaw off his own captured limb. But I knew it was neither.

I walked over to the kitchen door and pushed open the screen, stepped out onto the verandah and listened intently. Again, the sound trembled through the air. Despite its animal-in-distress quality, I knew Charlie Johnston served as the source of that outcry.

Charlie, like a lot of the local boys back in '14 had signed up to defend our country and way of life against the Prussian scourge that threatened to take over the free world. The young, idealistic Charlie that boarded a ship in Halifax was not the same Charlie that the army returned to his family at the end of the conflict four years later. Not by a long-shot. Of course, nobody who ventured overseas came back unchanged. How could you if you were involved in The Great War, the war to end all wars as it was billed.

Still, the changes in Charlie were much more profound than those in any of the other boys who lived to come home to our village again. Shell-shocked was the common description of the old folks who recollect the days of the war better than I did. I was only four when the war broke out, and eight when it finally ended. My recollections were more stories heard than things remembered.

They said Charlie had seen too much, done too much and heard too much to ever be sane again. And as a result, everyone sort of forgave his erratic actions. I did my best to be that understanding as well, but when Charlie got under the railroad bridge and started howling and baying like a wild animal, as I said earlier, it made me shudder. It might not have been actual fear, but it came darn close.

Charlie led the hobo life long before knocking on strangers' doors looking for food became as popular as it did in the Thirties. His family—brothers, sisters, aunts and uncles, his parents had died—tried their best to care for him. They would feed him when they could lure him into their houses. They would give him shelter if they could convince him to stay. That was the challenge.

Charlie didn't like confined spaces and he didn't really trust anyone. No one ever knew exactly what events Charlie had experienced during The Great War. It was just generally accepted that they had been traumatic.

He had a band of ribbons sewn on his tunic jacket. A couple of local men who know about such things said they were awarded for bravery under fire. No one ever saw any of the medals that went with those ribbons. Charlie never talked about any of it. His shoulder-flashes indicated he served with the Nova Scotia Rifles. That would explain a lot.

My uncle was also a member of the 25th Battalion, their official name. He didn't talk much about the war either. I know that of the original thousand members who fought for a year in Belgium, nine hundred were either killed, captured or injured. From there they fought in the Battle of the Somme, Vimy Ridge and Passchendaele among others. By the end of the war fifty-three percent were injured and fourteen percent, seven hundred and eighteen souls, died in battle. I can only guess what Charlie must have seen and endured.

Be that as it may, when Charlie started baying under the railway bridge, you knew that within an hour or so he would be knocking on your door. The Depression was actually a good thing for Charlie. This going door to door for food became accepted by most folks as times became tougher and Charlie simply fell into line with the other 'bos lining up at strangers' houses for meals. People became less scared of him.

I turned back into the kitchen and started frying up a couple of eggs. I would have the sandwiches made before Charlie got there. He would not be coming into the house like the other 'bos. He never did. And, if you took too long preparing something for him to eat, he might be gone when it was ready. Charlie marched to his own drummer and that drummer played erratically.

When the howling finally stopped, I noticed my father coming down from the barn. He always met Charlie in the driveway when he was home. I took the sandwiches out, gave them to Dad, and went back into the house to watch.

Dad calmly sat on the back step and waited. When Charlie arrived, he indicated a spot on the step and paused until Charlie joined him. He then offered Charlie one of the sandwiches and took a bit out of the other one himself. He spoke to Charlie in a low, murmuring voice. Charlie's head nodded up and down and he mumbled a few words back.

I don't know if my dad had any idea what

Charlie was saying or not. I had heard Charlie talk on a few occasions and most of what was being said had to be guessed at by his facial expressions and body actions.

Dad patted his shoulder, gave him the second sandwich from which he had taken a bite and together they got to their feet. The two of them walked quietly down the driveway until they reached the top of the hill where it sharply dropped off. Then, Dad reached out, took Charlie's had and shook it once, firmly.

Charlie gave a nod and then walked briskly, almost proudly, down the path for a few steps. Then, he slowed down, stooped a little and resumed his usual shuffle.

My dad never told me what transpired between the two of them at these occurrences. I can only guess. But, whatever it was, for a few very brief seconds, I knew Charlie felt good about himself again. I also knew that whatever hell he had gone through, I should be thankful for men like him. Depression or not, he had made the world a better place for people like me.

ABOUT THE AUTHOR

Besides writing short stories, Art Burton writes mystery novels. To date six are available:

For Hire, Messenger of God

Caught in the Line of Fire

Concealed From Sight

The Bag of Money

The Poker Game

The Independent

All of his books are available at the Nova Scotian libraries in HRM and Colchester East Hants.

For more information of these books and other short stories that are only available as ebooks, goto:
artburton.ca

Art lives with his wife, Flame, and hobo dog, Charley in Latties Brook, Nova Scotia

Email him at: art@artburton.ca